DISPATCH FROM EVERY SECOND GUESS

DISPATCH FROM EVERY SECOND GUESS

a verse memoir

Megan Gannon

DZANC BOOKS

DZANC
BOOKS

2580 Craig Rd.
Ann Arbor, MI 48103
www.dzancbooks.org

DISPATCH FROM EVERY SECOND GUESS. Copyright © 2025, text by Megan Gannon. All rights reserved, except for brief quotations in critical articles or reviews. No part of this book may be reproduced in any manner without prior written permission from the publisher: Dzanc Books, 2580 Craig Rd., Ann Arbor, MI 48103.

First Edition: March 2026
Cover design by Shelby DuVall
Interior design by Michelle Dotter

ISBN: 9781938603761

No part of this book may be used or reproduced in any manner for the purpose of training large language models, artificial intelligence technologies or systems.

Printed in the United States of America

10   9   8   7   6   5   4   3   2   1

*For Lauren, Manny, and Silas
And for Jeremy—all of it.
Always.*

*A lifetime is not so long.
You cannot wait for a tool without blood on it.*

—*Joseph Beuys*

DISPATCH AS PROLOGUE OR EPILOGUE

Every beginning is arbitrary, every
end a fiction. Start with your first

poor decision, or back further, start
with the woman whose daily

whittling/belittling taught you
you'd better be smart, at least.

Start with the man you might have been
happy with, if happiness was what

you'd wanted, poet at twenty-two. Start
with the first man to show you your every

pore was a mouth open to more flesh.
Start with that darkness where you felt

your skin dissolve. Start with your fear
of being lost, then finding that the day

to day sameness was how you'd become
unseen. Start with the third time

you told your husband, "Every time
I see you like that, a little of my love for you

dies." Start with the moment you realized
his *good enough* for you wasn't *good enough*

for the son you'd been given by another woman.
Start with the years when you mistook

silence for peace, when so much
nothing almost crushed you,

when you could never fill the house
with enough noise to feed your boy.

Start with the man you couldn't resist.
Start with the way he bent time to hold you

in a full waiting breathlessness. Start
with the small cracks and breaks. Peace

was never what you wanted, was it?
Now you'll never run out of artifacts

to sift through, never dig deep enough
to unearth every shard. You were hurt,

and now you've done some of the hurting.
It all begins with wanting, with finding

yourself wanting. Start there.

CONTENTS

Dispatch as Prologue or Epilogue	09
Dispatch with Storm Warning	13
Dispatch from the Years Yet Childless	15
Dispatch from a Viral Video	16
Dispatch from the First Year Alone	18
Dispatch from the Kmart Party Aisle	20
Dispatch from the Hotel Pool	23
Dispatch from the Ars Poetica	26
Dispatch from a Petit Prelude	28
Dispatch from a Failed Long Distance	29
Dispatch from the Middle Distance	31
Dispatch from a Familiar Fairy Tale	33
Dispatch from a Memory of Mint	35
Dispatch as an (Almost) Epithalamium	36
Dispatch from the Month Before Your Arrival	38
Dispatch from an Innocent Request	40
Dispatch from Your Fourth Month	42
Dispatch from Simultaneous Swim Lessons	43
Dispatch from Another Familiar Fairy Tale	45
Dispatch from That Day in Door County	47
Dispatch Four Days After the Funeral	48

Dispatch from a New York Times Article the Day Mary Oliver Died	51
Dispatch from the Cusp of 2020	53
Another Dispatch from the Familiar Fairy Tale	54
Redacted Dispatch with Parenthetical Hindsight	55
Dispatch from the Missing Police Report	57
Dispatch for My Nephew's Last Two Girlfriends	60
Dispatch from Advanced Poetry	62
Dispatch from My Internalized Misogyny	63
Dispatch from the Domestic Interior	64
Dispatch from Quarantine	66
Dispatch from My Oldest Son's Greatest Love	67
Dispatch as a Late-Addition Ghazal	69
Dispatch from the Manuscript's Every Second Guess	70
Dispatch from the Unwritten	73
Dispatch from a Necessary Request	75
Dispatch for the Third Person	77
Dispatch as an Almost-Apology	81
Dispatch from the Fairy Tale's Retelling	82
Dispatch Walking Past the House I Was Outbid On	83
Dispatch to the Crone	85
Dispatch on the Golden Ratio	87
Dispatch Halfway Up the Summit	89
Dispatch on Etymology	91
Dispatch on the Obvious	92

DISPATCH WITH STORM WARNING

Suddenly restlessness
had a weather—summer, season of skin

and unfettered breath, of whole lives
devoured between pages. We failed

each other in ways we could
and could not control. So much undone

by proximity—home from work, closer, too close—
how the cloud-cover drew on and stripped us

of all intention, attention at loose ends,
astray. The sight of green sprawling in all directions

made me want to spread myself thin,
arms hooked around both ends of the horizon,

cumulus blooms over a slow cobra of smoke.
I became her, battering to tatters,

this lady of the darkening margins.
Tuned to ruination, she twirled, and where

she touched a toe down: dust lifts, debris.
Strand of dark yarn, twitching umbilicus

dropped from a womb-dark cloud—how long
before she pulled apart, and where

she dissipated, light sifted in among flung dust.
It was this in me above all else that he tied to,

this sight that consumes all the life-lived
detritus: that stranger's eyes, bright

as standing water, those bedhead mussed curls,
that baby's dimpled shoulders, freckled elbows,

hands that never fully unclench from a fist—
all I could not have and had no claim on.

Anyone can tell you what becomes of hunger:
always the widening where the weather

comes from, the narrow throat making a mess
of its urgent searching, and the wanting

is the center of the still.

DISPATCH FROM THE YEARS YET CHILDLESS

In marrying, you make a gift of your life—I knew this—
but standing by the window-grimed light

above the sink, I could not bring myself to speak.
We do not live because others want us, but to feel

myself unseen by his facing gaze, unspoken to
by the mouth that pledged his always

was to feel myself dissipate like atoms from a glittering
center, light casting out for something to strike. Bodied,

but dissolved—the furthest ghost of his knowing.
I held the fork to the faucet water—the clear fall

of forgetfulness—my finger counting without looking
the sharp bite of the tines. The objects of his life

had become my company: the slack dishtowel,
the chipped-lip cup, the flat, empty faces of plates

waiting to hold something that might sustain me.

DISPATCH FROM A VIRAL VIDEO

The midwife is holding the babies' faces above water.
They don't know that they've been born; they are clenched

in a Gordian knot, arms entwined around necks,
legs bunched as tangled cord, their two heads pressed

cheek to cheek like tango dancers. Their bodies are deep
in the sink, the faucet pours over their eyes, and just their noses

and mouths breach the water, little dry islands
where the tide slowly recedes as the midwife lifts them.

I watch the YouTube video without any of the usual guilt.
I stood, fully clothed, at the foot of the bed in another bright room

as the doctor twisted my son's head like a doorknob
to wrest his shoulders from the body where he was emerging.

He was my son, and he was not yet my son, and all I could do
was watch. He is my son and some Christmases he visits

his half-brother and wrestles on the carpet with the one person
he looks like in all the world. Then he goes back to crashing

Hot Wheels and building Legos in my house or the apartment
his father moved into shortly before I called his birthmother

and listened as she said, *This isn't what I wanted for him.*
I almost picked another couple.

The midwife's wrists surface, the babies begin to twist, they are
waking without crying, which is what some people do every morning.

In the silence of my computer screen, no one says,
Welcome to the world, we have tried to ease you in, you are here

and you are wanted, but please know that unlike you
in this already-gone moment, no happiness in this life comes clean.

DISPATCH FROM THE FIRST YEAR ALONE

Weekends aren't weekends when you parent a child
who wants to know where you're going and when you'll be back

when you stand from your chair to get more coffee.
Thursdays I spend four hours thumbing books

of poems trying to find a room inside my head
and don't find it. Worry for my son is the silence inside

every room and the noise. The second night in a row
I get home to a babysitter and rush to hug him, he lets me,

limply, and won't meet my eye. Later I make him
laugh at the dinner table and realize if I can just stay

joyful every minute I'm with him I might successfully
irradiate the sadness from his bones with my love chemo.

For the first time in his life, I'm watching my child
accumulate little piles of grief and no amount of washing

over and over those shards will turn them dull and harmless
as sea glass. I try to stop flailing outward and get quiet,

sink down inside and trust a stillness will fill me
and hold me, half-drowned but breathing.

I want to believe drowning isn't even the right analogy—
something with cocoons instead—that the waiting

has a change at the end of it, but if the butterflies and moths
could talk they'd tell you that having your skin and insides

reduced to goo hurts worse than you first imagined. They'd say
there's pain until you don't have a body left to feel it with,

until the pain dulls down to an itch you can climb out of.

DISPATCH FROM THE KMART PARTY AISLE

I'm looking for favors for my son's seventh birthday
when I turn to find a bird sputtering against

the greeting card display. One wing bats askew but I
don't stop to think what this might mean when I

swoop in, scoop it up, pinning the good wing
against my palm. The bird is the color

of lint, its claws curl to fit like a ring, and its heart
beats hard as a finger would need to tap glass to get

my attention. I abandon my cart, walking quickly
through the automatic doors; I'm obviously

hiding something in my hands as I exit the store
but no one stops me. Outside, in the sudden sun,

I'm not sure what to do. I see a tree behind
the laundromat and walk toward it, then more trees

in the alley, so shift my trajectory. I'm making this up
as I go along, but I'm not thinking

how the bird is hurt, how I should do the hard work
of finding a shoebox and a nature center to save it.

I haven't even emptied my hands but already
I'm turning the bird into a metaphor, on this day

a second Black man—a stranger who is not (yet) my son—
was killed by police in twenty-four hours. All day I've been

fluttering the windows of my house or scrolling Facebook—
thumbs up, thumbs up, angry emoji, repost—and midway

through the day I find I've done nothing. Some days
after a shooting I can keep myself focused and productive,

but today the numbers matter and maybe if there had been two
birds I'd have gone to the trouble of saving them, but just one

bird I carried into the tall grass. I opened my hand
and stroked the bird's head and wing until its eye flickered

and closed. Its heart had grown quiet, and for a moment
I thought it felt safe in my fist, but then I realized

it might be dying from shock and terror as I tried
(not very hard) to help. Please, there is no metaphor here.

The cop who shot Philando Castile wasn't trying to help him.
Castile's girlfriend couldn't help him as he bled out beside her

because her daughter was in the backseat and she knew
if she tried to touch her love the cop would shoot her too.

No metaphor, even though my son is turning seven,
and it's a lucky number. He is the Black boy

with a white mother who makes white strangers feel less racist
for loving him so easily. On his fourth birthday a jury acquitted

Trayvon Martin's murderer, but there is no metaphor
for worrying about how tall he is for his age.

I tried to help the bird and, instead, killed it more quickly.
When I got home I thought, *bird flu,* and washed my hands.

DISPATCH FROM THE HOTEL POOL

In between days at the Magic Kingdom and Universal
Studios, we take a break from the crowds and lines

to lounge by the hotel pool: two sisters, a boy apiece,
hers from her belly and pale as our DNA, mine

too golden to have anything to do with me.
Above and below, the sky and water are the same

perfect shade of maybe-I-can-catch-my-breath-between-
water-basketball-and-mama-lookits, maybe my son

won't need me to wade in and attend to him if another kid
will splash in the shallow end with him. Thank you,

little blonde girl, whose mother five minutes later
calls her over, says something sternly, then sends

her off to the opposite end of the pool. Thank you,
little blonde girl, for glancing back at my Black son

and slowly over time floating back over, jumping with him
again and again into water clearer than any mirror

her mother has ever looked into before she calls
her daughter over and scolds her, sends her elsewhere.

I put down my book and consider strolling over
to that other mother, all smiles, asking is there

a problem, introducing myself and my son, but then I think
of the moms who can't stroll over in way-too-much white skin

to convince another white lady their son's okay, how just the act
of walking over sells out women whose great-grandmothers

were sold too many times. So I sit tight, simmer, watch
that other mother's assumptions swirl my son like clouds still

too far out from shore to signal danger. For now, just
two children crouched side by side on the ledge

of the shallow end, when another girl runs up, bumps my son,
sends him dominoing into the blonde girl who topples in

and comes up crying. I'm up, finding my flip-flops, but already
the other mother is clearing a storm path, picking up my son

under the armpits and flinging him—without looking where
or how he'll land—across the concrete. And now I know

I could touch a stranger with both hands—will—but halfway
across the cement I see my son has landed on his bottom,

surprised but unhurt, as I reach the woman who yells
back above my screaming, "I'm sorry, I misunderstood!"

You misunderstood? 1) That my child is worth something?
2) That your daughter's brand of golden isn't worth more?

3) That if you hover like a harpy for hours waiting for something
bad to happen at the hands of my son that eventually anything

bad that happens will be (you think) at the hands of my son?
He is safe, I am shaking and he is laughing—not sure why

that lady touched him or why I'm paler than usual. And I see
how I'll do things differently from now on: for his sake

I'll step in, flash my too-white smile and send up a silent
apology to all the Black mothers of Black sons I'm betraying

as I try to convince another white woman that this one, my son,
he's all right. (But also this one. And this one. This one. This.)

DISPATCH FROM THE ARS POETICA

I would like to be more generous to you. I imagine you want
to see past the curtains holding the light between cloud-passes,

outside to the branches where buds of *nature's first green-gold*
are slowly unclustering. I would like to give you

sounds to carry around like a pilot light that sputters in your gut
as you navigate the sidewalk-gray day, but how can I name

the spring leaves without also mentioning the brown tatters
of seed strings, too damp and tangled to flutter or fall, clumped

like a scum on the wind-riffled limbs? Here is the problem:
I need to write the things I don't want to say, to lay them out

austere and unpretty as snowfall on an airport parking lot.
I need to say my ex-husband is hiring a young, pretty poet

for the job he'd never have hired me for when we were married,
and though I do not want him, I would like some assurance

that he is not worthier of finding someone to love than I am. You see,
I have a talent for saying ugly things, and I cannot give you

what you want any more than I can avoid dribbling coffee
on the sides of this white mug. I could say "tracked like rain-stains,"

but there is nothing sublime in smelly smears left by this mouth
of mine that fails to catch every drop of what the rest of me needs.

In this house I live in, the mirror holds a blank face to empty rooms
and the best I can do is tell you it does nothing but let the light pass.

DISPATCH FROM A PETIT PRELUDE

The span of my hand from G to E could cup the skull
of an infant. A finger dropped to D could stroke an ear

or snare a curl, ring for my empty finger. From G to F
I'm spanning shoulder blades, taking their tender measure,

but G to G requires another body—how I might touch
under thumb and pinkie the two charge points at either end

of a lover's collarbone—and now when my hand contracts
it holds breath and heat above the caged beating.

I don't know how to touch one thing without
the ghost of all I've wanted aching in my tendons.

I don't know how to have one feeling, clean and precise
as the rain outside diminuendoing leaves only seems to be.

This shift from major to minor key I only ever hear
as light going into hiding. I can't have everything

I want at once, but I can hold their many absences,
wooden casing trembling with trapped sound.

DISPATCH FROM A FAILED
LONG DISTANCE

There's little natural precedent for what I asked of him:
moths to the flame, sure, and certain domesticated dogs

will lick themselves raw. Some creature must eat the fruits
of cacti, swallowing slicing spines along with liquid light,

but most of us choose sweetness unmitigated by barbs—
honeyed and wholly gold. Still, pain is inversely proportional

to any grabbed happiness, maybe, or pleasure is itself
a kind of pain, and pain a sharp release from that searing bright.

I might have asked him to be brave, though I've never met
another human who would risk ash for this brief burn

of phosphorus-white. I think since we're here, we might as well
feel. The pond's unblemished skin ruptures predictably in patterns

that disappear before they still. Rivers swallow in dirty rills
what's given to them and keep running where land allows.

I didn't want us to be bounded water.
There is an ocean that won't go away outside his window.

It never stops feeling in white flinches, never stops mawing,
mawing at the ragged shore. See how its many mouths

are shattered glass at this distance: glass ground down
to glitter, now part of the sand—unthinking—and wanting more.

DISPATCH FROM THE MIDDLE DISTANCE

Having survived the wreckage of two marriages,
we arrive at this late morning in middle age

bright-eyed and intact. Alive and needing
nothing, we laze the wide, white beach of my bed—

this island of found hours—our words
more careful than our mouths. In the silence

of the empty house, we don't speak
of our children's grief, of the ways we weren't

enough for our spouses but would have stayed
anyway. We see how we've been freed by debris.

Here, in the quiet of the workday, your face—
a marvel of lived-life and laugh-lines—

hangs for limitless minutes in the air above me.
I trace the cherry blossoms inked on your forearm

and a smile blooms between us; I close my eyes
as the sympathetic sun breaks from behind clouds.

Someday—later, we will speak of it—we will travel
to Japan, where we can wander through petal-light

and the silence of combed stones, together
in a country where the beauty in brokenness

isn't just an idea, but a bowl mended with gold
we can hold in our hands and lift to our lips.

DISPATCH FROM A FAMILIAR FAIRYTALE

Of all her father's children, she looks most
like her mother. She is so white she hovers

the room like moonlight. She wears
her uncombed hair like a crown,

mismatches her socks on quirky purpose.
She keeps her storybooks pristinely lined—

read, but spines unbroken—and asks me
to pick the pink for the page she's coloring.

She asks for cookies and waits for them
to be plated, seals her lips against the wrong kind

of fries, holding dinner hostage. Sometimes
she answers my "good morning"; sometimes, walking,

we each catch one of her father's hands, until I let go
and she wedges in to hold the hand I held.

She sleeps with the kitten I bought her,
kissing the tender pads of its paws.

She registers rage as a funneling silence,
watches zombie movies without a flicker of fear.

She has a heart like mine, I think, though
I can't be sure. No way to check.

DISPATCH FROM A MEMORY OF MINT

Into the damp white light of those Mother's Day Sundays
my sister and I would rise, steal through the property-line

pines, and tear thin tongues of nose-tingling green
from the neighbor's garden. I imagine our two rounded

backs, curled like witches tending their brew,
our nightgowns damp at the hem from being dragged

through dew. I held my hands open for the offering
as my sister plucked piles of the fleshed, fluffy feathers

I'd cup to my chest. Back in the still-sleeping house,
we'd scoot curdled eggs around a hot pan, scrape

butter across toast, pour water that could burn us
to brew the tea our mother mixed with two pink packets

of fake sugar, our garnish mint rimmed around the waiting plate
like miscolored rays of a make-believe sun. How did we learn

such nurturing, in the absence of an inverse? My sister showed me
where the mint grew and how to take it, how to hold each

tiny blade gently, the serrations so small you could touch them
again and again without feeling cut.

DISPATCH AS AN (ALMOST) EPITHALAMIUM

How would we do it, and why, our hearts grown
gray-haired, crisscrossed with spider threads

as I used to imagine my innards were
before our son began to grow there. Do we do it

for him, pretend a party and some rings mean
two people make a cradle unbreakable

when we both know the bough breaks as it broke
for each of our other children?

Not in a church. Neither of us believes any power
higher than ourselves will see us through.

Not with the forty-dollar-a-plate reception
for loved ones who are too many assembled

in one place to talk to. Not with anyone, maybe,
but us two, not even our children, not even

this not-yet one who makes us one
in his almost-body as long as we both (or he)

shall live (long shall he live). Only you, me,
and some trees, mountains making the air

wide enough to breathe for a long time if not
forever. Not with vows or even words,

but you looking into me outside time
as you do sometimes—exasperated with my

self-quibblings, wordless in the after-love—
a returned gaze that doesn't flinch or clock

itself, but waits for what we can be to each other
in the always-lost-but-somehow-still-lasting-now.

DISPATCH FROM THE MONTH BEFORE YOUR ARRIVAL

I've been spending most mornings on my hands and knees
pulling weeds. Into the wet ground I gouge

with a metal prong and the serrated leaves come up
in bunches, clustered to a soft white root, tinged red.

I throw each little pompom aside and start in on another.
I wanted the yard tidy, but I also thought that shifting

the weight off my spine would allow you enough room
to flip head down inside this hammock of skin and muscle,

the way you should have by thirty-six weeks.
Your father jokes you have his stubbornness, but who

could deny this in a baby who made himself ten years after
either parent had any notion of him—ten years after my longing

conjured your brother from another woman's
body, ten years after your father sealed his insides

(he thought, forever) against the fertile well of your sister's
mother? You want to be here, and you don't care where

they have to cut me open to pull you into the waiting air.
I knew your dad a year when you took root—not quite

long enough for the many green fingers of his unhappiness,
those persistent habits I'd like to go after, too, at the root—

to show above ground. But how much of his morning
sullenness—the unseen dishes or piled laundry, the talk

of running away alone to the mountains—do I ignore,
thinking these aren't the kind of weeds connected

each to each by one long taproot? Which are the sulfurous,
yellow markers announcing themselves in plenty of time

to attack before they go to seed, and how many do I leave
alone as part of the season's green? You won't get grace

from me, baby. Before you're here for me to tend
and prod and coax and prune, I need to know whether

I'd be better letting it all go, becoming one of these other
mothers who willingly leaves her book facedown

in the sunshine to clap a little body down a slide, who chases
and pushes and swings her child with so much effort

that looks like love. Who will go home and silently
fold the empty shapes of clothes in on themselves, rinse

the dregs of morning from a husband's mug,
who will accept the bouquets of eely stems and furred,

pollened heads, vasing them again and again
in fresh water—knowing they're weeds, but weeds

she'll accept as long as they last from certain dirty hands.

DISPATCH FROM AN INNOCENT REQUEST

Answer: depends. Are you the mother
of this baby? Sibling? Grandparent? Father?

Are you anyone at all to this baby other than
the strange woman who keeps asking to hold him

even after the baby's mother has told you no? Okay,
that's not fair. You're no stranger. You are the woman

the baby's mother has carefully, concertedly vilified.
You are the woman who once threw a shoe

at the baby's father's head, the woman who missed
and broke a window instead. And sometimes,

when the baby's mother feels her rage at the baby's father
building like a tide rushing in to subsume her,

the baby's mother wants a shoe to throw too.
You are the woman the baby's father took to Paris

three times, the reason he lies awake most nights
calculating how to climb out of the debt

dea(r)th you dug with him. You are the woman
he left and kept coming back to over nineteen years

of his long life, the woman who cried the first time
you saw the baby's father holding him and proclaimed

the baby's existence "so weird" because he isn't yours.
He isn't yours. You are the baby's sister's absent mother,

the woman who offers parenting advice although you
only parent when you need Instagram to witness

you took the baby's sister for a bike ride. You are
the reason, perhaps, the baby's sister doesn't want much

to do with any kind of mother. You are not
the baby's mother, but the baby's mother

feels you in the emptiness she shapes her life around.
The baby's mother is busy holding back the you

she might turn into, so please understand, no,
for the last time, no, you cannot hold

the one person you've left untouched.

DISPATCH FROM YOUR FOURTH MONTH

Outside, bright leaves batter the window screens.
Here, you are a warm weight pinning me

to now. We will never be cleaner to each other.
You have yet to scrape the flint of your will

against mine, I have yet to hurt you
with my fervent need to make you always kind.

Sometimes on purpose we won't be what the other
wants, and part of me will curl like matchstick char.

I know what's coming, and all I can do is sit
with you through these wind-pummeled days

when all you need—breast, shoulder, capable hands—
I give and you receive without the spark of words.

These hours escape us as we sit huddled around
our double warmth: my palm fitted to the perfect globe

of your skull, the worm-pull of your need
burying its head deep inside my left breast.

DISPATCH FROM SIMULTANEOUS SWIM LESSONS

On Tuesdays the baby licks the balcony viewing window
as his brother and sister swim in side-by-side lanes.

His sister is deep within herself, adjusting goggles
over eyes that cannot see us a story above her head.

Her dive is all toes, her stroke all elbows that softly
dent the water. As she sends the bone-white reed

of her body dutifully down the length of the pool,
her hair pulses like a jellyfish bell behind her.

When she hauls herself free, shivering, the waterlogged
cloth sags, and soon she'll ask for a new suit with more

padding to cover what's budding. She has completed
one lap, one more chore crossed off between her

and the next day's list of to-dos. One lane over,
the baby's brother throws his goggles into the deep end

so he'll have to jump in to retrieve them before his teacher
says it's time. His dive is a careening comet screaming

cowabunga, his feet a ceaseless motor that churns
his joy so high it rains down on every lane. His wet curls hang

clumped as uncarded wool, dripping chlorine
he blinks and licks away as he waves and mouths words

over his teacher's talking. I waggle the baby's hand
back at him and think how, even from this height,

and through such clear elements, I cannot discern
who I'm more frightened for: the baby's sister and brother

each marked as prey by their bodies—her, by her
imagined weakness, him, by his supposed strength.

And indeed, her body is thin and breakable and flowering.
And indeed, his body is brown and glossy with the energy

of ten suns. And the baby is a pale reflection floating
above them, swimming his arms through unresisting air.

DISPATCH FROM ANOTHER FAMILIAR FAIRY TALE

We did not abandon them there, though it was my idea:
the two of them alone together in the wilds

of a Midwest shopping mall at Christmas, not holding
hands but bound by their word and the rareness

of the occasion to stick together. In the event
of an emergency they have her cell phone,

his maleness, their long-limbed, always-competitive
swiftness to get them to safety. Each of them

with a few folded bills—the crumbs we have left
to give them—in their pockets to buy gifts with.

They wander the well-marked paths of plateglass,
weaving between the carts of overpriced sweatshirts

and magical skin creams, scented squishies
and cat calendars trying to prepare us all for what's coming.

Light glitters in every window, warring music wafts
from every escape route, and if an evil shows up to spew

its black spit at them, I've told them both to run and not
look back—leave each other behind if they have to—loyalty

and bravery and cunning and all those fairytale virtues
saving no one in this age of senseless storylines.

DISPATCH FROM THAT DAY IN DOOR COUNTY

That day you stood, wordless and waist-high in waves, and held me
with the help of water. Hours earlier, I sat in the car scrolling

my phone when a message appeared from an old friend
with the name of a mutual—I'll call him *friend*—the word *accident,*

the words *call me,* so I did, and she answered sobbing. What
to do on that unexceptional Sunday, our kids already swim-suited

and seat-belted, but *go on, go on,* and drive to Door County.
The rest of the ride silent except for my sounds, no one sure

if they're allowed to have fun until they're finally loosed
to the shadow-sharp air, their calls and accidental laughter

high as the wind-buoyed gulls. Me, beached by the unspoken
book swelling, word-clogged, inside me. So many of us

when faced with a loved one's grief for a past lover would go
cold, step away, but you pulled me into the shifting,

bone-tightening, mid-September lake and lifted me, bride-like.
I fit my face against your collar bone. Around us, a fathomless blue,

a rustling in the far ring of trees, and you at the center cradling
the weight inside me, holding me up against the onslaught of horizon.

DISPATCH FOUR DAYS AFTER THE FUNERAL

I might as well mourn the man-boy in twenty-
year-old pictures who was only mine for a few months

(if at all) as much as the man he became far away
in the meantime—same tanned, Clark Kent face,

same warm-throated laugh, same hundred images
stilled in a golden-remembered glow. But then

he became someone else's husband, father to the two
seemingly bored kids I watched throwing wakeboards

into his sister's pool the day before his funeral.
The way I used to search crowds for his flip-flopped

swagger, I now watch hungrily as his son and daughter
demonstrate they might be okay someday.

Truly, I gave him up long ago—it feels
like stealing to try to remember what I almost loved—

now that my love for another resides in my chest
like a thirst or caught breath, a full emptiness I press

every night against this warm body filled with another
life's echoes. Now that half of my grief is for the wife

who loved him twenty times longer and legally,
now that she'll have to weather the couples-get-togethers

and suspicions of male friends' wives, and all with no warning.
I want to send her something from my years

as a single mother, maybe the moment I'd finally
whittled myself and my child into something spare

and hard in our matter-of-fact unbending. It will be
who-knows-how-many days until she can find

that heartwood—a number that waits in her
future the way this death waited in numbered days

past the days I knew him. But no, I don't believe
our endings wait like a stopped clock, that the boy

who slammed his truck into a man on his morning run
had that act encoded in him since birth, any more

than the woman who ran up and watched the light
leave those eyes had that moment waiting to define her—

but it does. His death came at her from both sides
of time and stilled her in that moment as she wrapped

a T-shirt around his head, the same way I hover over the day
years ago he gouged himself on a broken branch and I helped

hold a T-shirt to his skull to stanch the flow. I don't
believe one moment made the other, but they call

to each other across the distance of our breath:
the moment I first wondered, his blood on my hands,

if I'd ever want to call him mine, calling to the moment
he became no one's, staining a stranger's hands.

DISPATCH FROM A *NEW YORK TIMES* ARTICLE THE DAY MARY OLIVER DIED

—with lines from her poems

In a small city in Italy, a woman removes her shoes,
cups them to her chest, and tiptoes the cobblestone streets.

Dogs are carried on their walks. Neighbors greet each other
with sudden smiles, a jerky wave, then pass in silence.

What more could I do with wild words?
Coffee shops set cups into saucers lined with napkins,

and in the museum behind five blocks of blocked-off streets
the instruments someone deemed mankind's most

precious are being played for eight hours, six days a week.
I want to believe that the imperfections are nothing—

that inside the building, the air crouches in darkened ducts.
A light bulb buzzes, and a velvet glove reaches up to untwist it.

Microphones, sensitive as telescopes trained on space,
are tuned instead to our human gasps and tappings,

(and what has consciousness come to anyway, so far?)
to the rasp of horsehair across catgut and a sound

too rich for most ears to distinguish from a violin
made last year in a factory. This is how we are as humans:

someone with sharper senses tells us to look, listen,
to learn something by being nothing,

and we trust them to know what will make us whole.
The recordings will be digitized and broken, new music

constructed from the pieces of arpeggios played
by instruments soon too brittle to be touched.

Is it necessary to say any more?
The instruments will be laid in their soft cases.

The pegs will slowly loosen their precise tuning,
and the stillness inside the holes the shapes of seahorses

will make a music none of us can hear—or bear to hear—
tending, as all music does, towards silence.

DISPATCH FROM THE CUSP OF 2020

The best you is a water-image, a shimmer simmering
just outside your line of sight. She shines with a secret

some might misname wisdom, but wisdom
is a storm cloud, forking dendrites of flashing tongues,

and the best you chooses where to turn the pinpoint
of her gaze, boring, ignoring her way like a bee

inside the self-made sweetness of ignorance.
The future does not lie outside the beloved's orbit,

but the best you plots her trajectory, bent on survival,
circling, always skirting just outside this event horizon.

ANOTHER DISPATCH FROM THE FAMILIAR FAIRY TALE

The princess is bent on disappearing. Locked
in her room from the inside, she emerges

at odd hours, her hair a tangle to match the knot
she's picking within herself. The queen has tried

giving her the room with the better view, rousing her
mornings with soft words, but loving the child

grants her no ownership. The queen could be
made of glass. Only the king can conjure a greeting,

a glance. The princess reduces her body to transparency,
all the better for her father to find and unravel the snare

she's bent on tightening. He will allow no one
near her, having cobbled together a clear coffin

for the girl to live in—all the better to protect her
from words that might reach her—all the better

to keep the tendrils of the tangle from escaping.
The queen would pry the lid and shake the girl

awake. Yet she can do nothing, sitting day after day
asking a window grown opaque with dust:

Am I fair? Am I being fair? Am I even here?

REDACTED DISPATCH WITH PARENTHETICAL HINDSIGHT

Because you asked the baby's older sister and brother to watch him
while you showered—fifteen minutes, max. Because the baby's brother

went outside, leaving the baby's sister to [make a mistake].
(Is it necessary to commit the details to poetry-posterity?

The important thing is how the adults around her reacted.)
Because, as you sat there listening to her blame her mistake

on the boy she lives with (as any child might), you looked
to her father and knew he would say nothing.

Because you knew if you said something to the baby's sister,
that the baby's father would scold you for upsetting her.

Because, (your rage told you,) the baby's sister is white
and the baby's brother is Black, the brother's blamed.

Because you sat there, anger funneling into a dark, hard pit.
Because the next day you left and took the boys with you.

Because the next day a white woman walking her dog
in Central Park was asked by a Black man to leash her dog.

Because in a city of six million people, where a man is trying
to find a sliver of quiet in which to hear a bird's dark, jagged call,

this seemed a reasonable request. Because the white woman
did not appreciate the correction. Because the white woman

called the police. Because the white woman told the police
that an African American man was threatening her.

Because the white woman knew she could pin her own
poor behavior on the Black man and come out clean—oh so

lily white. Because rage seeped from your pores like rancid onions
for weeks. (Because your anger will tell you what you want

to hear, will allow you to imagine connections, to miscast
a little girl's wrong.) Because *personal* and *political* begin and end

the same way. Because this story always begins and ends
the same way. Because the white woman learned her righteousness

somewhere. Because she learned it under your roof.

DISPATCH FROM THE MISSING POLICE REPORT

Five eighteen-year-olds squished in the backseat
of an Uber. Short ride back from a party. Plenty

of smack-talking, posturing about who can bench
how much in their what-sized T-shirts, when my nephew's

best friend grabs my nephew's head and slams it
into the window. When the car stops suddenly/finally

in the destination driveway and the riders spill out,
my nephew's best friend hauls him by the neck

back into the car, jabs his thumbs into my nephew's
eye sockets. When someone yanks my nephew

by the ankles to pull him from the pummeling,
my nephew's best friend pins him, grabs my nephew

by the hair and bashes his face again and again into the cement.
Only when someone's mother opens her window

and yells about the noise does my nephew's best friend
relent. What's missing from the missing police report

is the information that my nephew's best friend
was one week away from leaving for college,

that all the stupid grief this culture wouldn't let
either boy process was coursing through his veins

along with a decent amount of alcohol he was new to
(that he knew now he could not hold). What's missing

is the fact that one of the passengers was a messenger
from the best friend's future life, a boy he hoped

would become his frat brother, for whom some swagger,
perhaps, needed to be performed. That there was a girl in the car.

That some of the swagger might have been for the girl
sitting on another friend's lap. None of this is exceptional.

Boys in this country beat each other every day, and because
we don't tell boys it's okay to grab that face

and kiss it, they grind it into the concrete. I could end this poem
here. I would like to end the poem here. I too

watch the evening news and silently pray to the perpetrators
of petty crime, *please be white, please be white.*

I don't want to tell one more story that will make
a Black boy seem scary, that will get a Black man killed.

Telling you that my nephew is white and his best friend
is Black feels like the greatest act of violence committed

in this poem. And by telling you that my sister didn't/couldn't
file the police report, I look like one more white lady

invoking Black friends, one more white lady trying
to convince you she's One of the Good Ones. I'm not

writing this poem to reassert the old violence
against Black America and make this whole conversation

turn to ash on my tongue, but you need to know, if
my nephew's best friend had been white, we would have

burned his house to the ground. I'm telling you this because
even when my sister and I were so enraged we wanted

vengeance, we wanted *justice,* we wanted all the words
white people invented to wrest power from our own

powerlessness, a voice registered inside us:
Don't call the police.

(See: even when not wielding power, we retain it.)
I'm telling you this with all the helplessness of centuries

of misused voices and hands. I'm telling you this
so you can carry like a votive inside you the knowledge

that one young Black man made a mistake and lived.

DISPATCH FOR MY NEPHEW'S LAST TWO GIRLFRIENDS

I'd like to tell you, *forget him, move on, you're young,*
you can do better, but the truth is, you can't.

He had those baby blues and luminous smile
since the day he arrived, lightning bolt of pure nerve

no one knew was coming. He is every bit as golden
as he seems to be. He has rebounded, pick and rolled

off an age when his birthright was everything, to this age
when he has to ask for what he wants, just like the rest of us.

The rules have changed when we weren't looking, all the men
around him decry, but his parents taught him when

and how to not touch a girl. Listen, I too still love
a man whose every tendon and sinew is a proof

of mathematical perfection, whose path through this world
was laid like a carpet at his feet through parted seas.

I'm not sorry the rules have changed for him, or for you.
Our mothers raised us to trim and tame and arrange every

stray hair, and now we wake to a world where it's not enough
to be pretty. It's not enough for him, or for you. You can't want

another human so hard that losing him lands you in the hospital.
You can't keep craving the tips of his fingers on the flawed bones

of your face more than you crave something that will keep you
breathing. There's plenty of red inside you, so let it power

your own two feet. Cross the livid emptiness he's left behind
to an untouched, unruly country.

DISPATCH FROM ADVANCED POETRY

These poets know a thing or two I'd teach
about the ways to fashion pretty verse.

Assigned at birth a loaded "she," they each
have learned the ways to shape their forms, or worse,

disfigure them. "Trim it back," I preach.
"Compress the language, find the poem's nerve."

The poets bow their heads to hear their speech
is better served by even fewer words.

The creeps and stalkers, man-splaining boyfriends—
the skin they've starved, carved, pickled, or plucked numb—

they won't redact, revise, or make amends
for penning down the violence, or succumb

to comeliness invented by old men.
They'll take up space and nurse the wordless hum,

and fuck whatever muse their form offends.

DISPATCH FROM MY INTERNALIZED MISOGYNY

I, too, see in Hillary Clinton my mother and so, like her less.
I, too, see in other women myself and so, like them less.

I wanted to be the one she'd admire enough to model
herself after. Now I'd settle for her eyes meeting mine.

When I spit another woman's name with the word *awful,*
I remember the bad taste comes from my own tongue.

I'm attracted to slight brunettes, women who resemble me outwardly.
I joke that my 10% bisexuality is actually a skewed narcissism.

There's only so long I can keep this skin taut. Even apples
left in the fridge wrinkle eventually around subcutaneous softness.

Seriously, enough with the botanical imagery. Women's bodies
don't exist to flower fleetingly before ripening into usefulness.

Once, I combed the girl's wet hair, and every time I hug
her father's head to my chest, I touch the ghost of those spider strands.

An image committed to paper is purged from the mind's eye,
but permitted to persist. To ignore is to repress, or to vanquish?

My espaliered/splayed apple tree hardens into the shape
it was tied to. No way to reclaim the wayward lushness of its early life.

DISPATCH FROM THE DOMESTIC INTERIOR

I'm not trading on my face. I've spent too long
trying to find a space inside myself

where the mice and spiders can creep
from the crevices and speak. It's dark

down here. Plenty of poets will tell you
about the light, the air outside that lifts

wisps of hair, the ways to make the surface
of your skin more porous. I'm here to take you

six feet deeper, to the fat-insulated pockets
of your body where you can knit the knots

of your grievances. Oh, let it all go, the bright poets
tell us, releasing their gossamers to the wind.

But the scraps and fabric, the broken bits
and detritus cobbled into new likenesses

are what I use to build my nest, where I curl
to lick myself raw and sharpen my teeth

for keening. I'm fed on these receipts.
Please know, the bodies you nurture will see you

and not see you. When you make yourself
indispensable, you make yourself invisible.

The curve of your neck into your shoulder
might as well be the swan-like shape

of a lampshade, just another household object
to be used and used up. They don't mean any harm.

They're not intentionally mistreating
a table when they leave rings.

DISPATCH FROM QUARANTINE

The real sickness is how quickly I sink into my own
worst version. The noise of bodies rustling these walls, calling

from other rooms to tend to them, leaving their trails
of spilled cereal, empty soda cups martialed on the counter

directly above the trashcan, toilet paper propped
on top of the old roll, little chaoses to be tidied.

(*Chaos* can't be plural, the dictionary tells me. *I can no longer
be singular,* I snap back.) A mother tried to abandon her son

at a park, and when he ran to the car to hitch a ride back home
she drove over him, then picked up his body and gave it a ride.

Like the accounts of loved ones dying alone in hospitals,
these stories leave me singing to the dark, *not me, not mine.*

I yelled at my son in the car so loud the neighbors turned to look
at the rolled-up windows as we drove past. I drew my rage

from the scrape-bottom dust of my lungs. I shrieked until his simpers
turned to cries and I kept screaming. I found air I never knew I had,

burned through it like toilet paper or some life-riskable need
you can buy more of if the stores have stock. In plagues past, the body

wept with sores. In this one, suddenly, we find we have no breath left.

DISPATCH FROM MY OLDEST SON'S GREATEST LOVE

He asked me once if I thought we're just *us* in heaven,
and because I'm not accustomed to lying, even to give comfort,

I told him *No. Your energy continues and joins
all the other atoms in the universe, but it's not* you.

Good, he relief-sighed. *I don't want to live forever. It sounds
so boring.* Every day during the pandemic he finishes

his schoolwork by three, snaps his laptop shut, then hops on his bike
and pedals hard for the chemical factory siding. He waits for hours.

Cars driving by sometimes roll down their windows to ask
if he's okay. He's okay. He'd be better if he could see his friends,

if his mother yelled less and listened more and maybe cooked something
different, if the days on days on days could offer some small surprise.

But this time is predictably his. It's late, and the sun is relentless,
when miles down the heat-wavered tracks a light turns red:

a pinprick approaches in the dimming of the day. It's the light
that reaches him first, then the rumble, and then

the train's assaulting every sense and cell, clacking
through rushing air and a whirl of hot wind, past where

he waits twenty feet back anchored under a shop awning.
It's not about thrill-seeking. He'd never be unsafe. He's the kid

who always took three attempts to brave a new slide, who only
this year learned to swagger abrasions, who helicopters

his baby brother's leaps and tumbles. Every day
in this sameness, he rushes towards something

immense and unstoppable, all that sensation echoing his chest
like a force he might have made himself that you can't fail

to hear. He can see it coming— it's overpowering—
and then—thank God—it's just over.

DISPATCH AS A LATE-ADDITION GHAZAL

Impossible calculus: would you be (in Milwaukee or Green Bay) safer amid Black faces, or will a buffer of white bodies help you stay safe?

No Nerf guns, no uncombed hair, no hoodies. No solo runs for Skittles, no solo runs ever. Not *sheltered*. Not *deprived,* per se. *Safe*.

Early pandemic days, what we can't see inside someone could kill you. School becomes your laptop. Every day unremarkable, gray, safe.

I'm not the only white woman watching you through curtains, but I'm eyeing every metal flash and gunned engine, keeping you—I pray—safe.

The motorist didn't think *Rail fan*. Didn't think *Calling cops could get a Black boy killed*. Saw a teenager, tracks. Thought *Better call. Play it safe.*

Summers you were little, you played tag across yards. Any porch was home base—Megan's son could touch any door and say *safe*.

DISPATCH FROM THE MANUSCRIPT'S EVERY SECOND GUESS

A person wants to stand in a happy place, in a poem.
—Mary Oliver

For starters, your Black son is never a *you*
in these poems. You other him to talk about racism.

Are you the white woman hoping to cash in
on the half-second when this country might

have given a damn about Black lives? Why do you let
this country turn your son into a third person?

(You went back and wrote that ghazal
for him when you realized the oversight. Admit it.)

You use *you* for the man, and the son you share,
and the woman you hate, and sometimes to distance

yourself from the *I* (as you do here). *You* is an intimacy
or a way to push away or a way to let yourself

off the hook. You should let some other people
off the hook. For instance, cut all the poems

about the girl. It's not fair to hold a child
accountable for her actions when she's in pain.

Kids should be off-limits in poems, unless
the poems are wholly affectionate.

You make her visible when the one thing
she wants is to remain unseen. Okay, so you document

your own unhappiness too—that doesn't give you the right
to write about hers. Did you have the right to demand

kindness from a child you lived with? You require
too much kindness. You require more kindness

from children than you require from yourself.
You should figure out how to require kindness kindly.

In kind. You're just reacting from your own well of hurt.
Sure, it was hard for you to live again with someone

who never left her bedroom—and when she did,
ignored you—but that girl isn't your mother. Maybe

it's her dad you're mad at. For not doing more
for her. For not shielding her from her own terrible

mother. But he can't give her more than he's been
given, more than he gives himself, and he gives himself

so little. Why always this obsession with airing
your grievances and your own ugliness?

You used to write pretty poems like Mary Oliver.
No one will call this book beautiful. Do you need

your poems to be beautiful? For far too long
your poems were one more glittery accessory,

one more gloppy cosmetic trying to convince yourself
you were worthy of attention. But poetry needs

to make room for all the feelings, doesn't it? Can poetry
treat meanness and keep breathing?

You want to believe you'll be forgiven
for what you've written, but you're not asking.

This poem isn't an apology. You should cut it.
You should cut all the poems. Only people

don't need permission to exist.

DISPATCH FROM THE UNWRITTEN

Some days my baby's fingers back and forth brushing
a blanket tag in the late summer, dusk-dappled light

are my poem; some days it's his brother's triumphant glance
back at my waiting car when the ghost-horn of a train echoes

his vigilance beside the still-empty track. There is more
than one way to make of this life a lasting. Forgive me

if the books I might have written linger like a miscarriage.
That word—as in *miscarriage of justice*—and what is justice now

that the surprise quickening of my youngest might have felt
less blessing than sentence. I had a choice, and still somedays

I lament the sentence I've been given and not given. Still,
I show him how to stroke rosemary—the word and the herb—

and hold that violet scent for hours. Still, I teach him to pluck
the mint and lay the leaf like a tongue on his tongue. Even childless

Dickinson must have lost the spider-gossamer of a line
to fingers sticky with bread dough. Even Woolf, kneeling

in the dirt to bury bulbs like landmines, must have felt
her shoulders brushed with the strobe-flash of a phrase.

Months later, all that deferred wonder gestating into longing,
green spearheads straining towards the ungoverned air.

DISPATCH FROM A NECESSARY REQUEST

I never know when I'll feel her over my shoulder—
the multiverse me who screamed in the firehouse

with the other unclaimed parents. Tonight,
for instance, when my forehead presses his cheek,

my mouth to his shoulder, my nose nuzzling his neck,
I feel her in that other hallway, hand on the doorknob

to a stale-aired version of this dark room.
Here, he snakes an arm under my chin,

my head locked in a thin vice as he knots knuckles
through my hair like hanging onto a net

for dear life. His very dear life. He knows
when I get to the words *Son, son, son, here it comes,*

to interrupt and ask if I'll stay
a little longer. He just watched me sing

a different song to his brother, scratching my fingers
through those tight, tangled curls, the affection

a teenager will allow. Three kisses brushed his forehead
before he turned his (daily widening) shoulder

to ward off more. Such a paltry smattering
compared to the tornado torrent I used to unleash

on his cheeks, nose, forehead, chin. He'd squinch
his eyes and let the rain of kisses fall. So yes,

I'll stay. I'll stay until my still-young son's limbs
twitch and jerk as he sinks into sleep, his slow

immersion into his own dreams
a small, nightly violence.

DISPATCH FOR THE THIRD PERSON

You do not have to be good.
You do not have to walk on your knees
for a hundred miles through the desert, repenting.
—Mary Oliver

When talk turns heavy and we can't keep
lifting our feet into a run, we start hiking.

The day dappling sunlight on our shoulders,
the air all around us wide and breathable, we think.

I say, maybe we could forgive ourselves
if we thought of ourselves in the third person.

Maybe you could forgive the kid so often left
to his own devices who, years later, will forgive himself

the almost burnt-down garage, the match-lit
locker, the thrown punches, and spitting in the face

of authority, but not the girl he took to the dance
and left there when he left with another.

Weekly, three decades later, you remember her
and wish for a cat-of-nine-tails to tear the guilt

from your skin. And maybe I could forgive
the girl who spent her whole childhood fighting

her mother's slights, who still can't bear an injustice
no matter who is wielding it. Maybe

I could forgive her for becoming the woman
who drove your daughter to middle school, and when

she refused again to get out of the car, left her there
in the parking garage and walked home.

Or maybe not. There's more to the story,
but there's no guilt a child can wield to make

that wrong seem right. And I'm not asking
some far-off, fictional reader to forgive

third-person me as much as I'm trying to find
a way to keep living inside this skin, keep picking

up these feet and breathing. Maybe
there's something wrong with the air.

As a country, we're not good
at forgiveness. Some of us don't know

how to forget and the rest of us forget what
we shouldn't, forget the harm

we've caused to pretend at our own
forgiveness. Almost daily I remember

the story of the father who forgot it was his day
to drop the toddler at school and drove to work

instead, his daughter silent and asleep
in the backseat where he found her again

at five o'clock in the hot parking garage, not asleep.
I wonder how you ever excise

that wrong, how you ever stop vomiting
as if to molt from the inside out your guilt-

ridden skin. Even in third person, I feel pity for the man,
but any forgiveness I can offer never reaches him.

And I'm not sure I want to forgive him.
My compassion for him is equal parts

revulsion for a grief that can't be purged.
Maybe he begged the judge to put him away.

Maybe in prison, the days upon days
of drudgery dwelling on your sins eventually

wears thin. Maybe we can't forgive in the abstract.
So I went to the mountains to run a hundred miles.

I drove my cramping, air-starved legs up crags
and passes, kicked toenails loose on loose rocks,

wrung every drop of salt from my muscles and kept
slogging through the looming darkness

until I felt I'd been punished enough. Enough
with the lack of compassion for the girl I imagine

resembles me, the girl I still carry inside the thin shell
of my girlhood like a nesting doll. There is no way to end

this poem in which so many children have been
harmed. There is no way to ask a self

for forgiveness, though I've tried. I only wanted
to keep your worst version company until

this relentless third degree heals your third-degree burn
into a third-degree crime and we've served our sentence.

DISPATCH AS AN ALMOST-APOLOGY

All my life I've coveted strangers' heirlooms: everywhere
the gold glints, snaking their curls, meshing with cells

made precious with the lavishness of mother-love. See
how it emboldens them to throw arms wide, the step-

lightness and eagerness for new because they know
they cannot lose, or if so, oh well. It's so easy to love

someone loved. All my life I've watched them
while linking metal ring to metal ring in shining

facsimile. The weight of it, carrying a self-love
that bites and pinches so no one can stab me through.

Even my own sons, coated in a golden glow I found
locked somewhere—shook free of dust to drape them in—

grow alien. Only this girl remains recognizable. Hiding
inside her chainmail, I poke to show she missed a spot.

DISPATCH FROM THE FAIRY TALE'S RETELLING

In another version I walk beside you, not pointing
out paths and commanding, *that one,* but keeping you

company beneath leaf-clatter and branch-tangles. I wait
for you to speak. Maybe I stop to cup a blowsy blossom

for you to sniff. You don't need to smudge your nose
with pollen—it doesn't mean I haven't shown you

a beauty that you don't have to make, or be.
Maybe you let me name things, or maybe

you're head down, trudging, keeping me always
a bend in the path behind. What happens when a howl

shivers the air cold? I can't imagine any version where I
don't bark back, spread my arms and let those teeth

rend meat, wet from my bones. But maybe the point is,
I can't be there. I didn't sew your red hood,

didn't pack your basket. You have to fill your own pocket
with stones, and when those run out, break the crust

of your only breakfast. The crumbs don't lead you home,
but onward, and I didn't even bake the bread.

DISPATCH WALKING PAST THE HOUSE I WAS OUTBID ON

In the four years since I settled for the grubby cottage
four blocks over, I've only ever driven past.

Tonight, both boys sleeping at the on-again
boyfriend's, I keep walking the dog around

snow-globe streets. We are the only ones out.
My relishing in fresh tracks is equal parts guilt

that neighbors will have to scrape their sidewalks.
The yellow house's three stories are still stately,

befitting a buyer who could match my asking-price offer,
but in cash. The generous front porch is still garlanded

and wreathed in mid-February. Prime packages
wait under a coating of snow. The lights are on

in only one of the four bedrooms, in the dark
square footage that might have been enough for us.

The truth is, I couldn't have afforded this house
on my own. We would have been stuck there,

each of us retreating to our ample bedrooms or haunting
the surgically bright remodeled kitchen in the wee hours.

In the cramped house I settled for, there was nowhere
to hide, and only those jaundiced walls, blotchy ceilings,

and dog-pee-palimpsested carpets could show
so clearly how little work we were able to do.

In the house I've leaned into loving, I breeze now, barefoot,
over refinished floors. I buy myself tulips. I sleep in the middle

of the bed in the middle of the house between two boys
who wake loving me enough to want my company. I dream singly.

I sit at the kitchen counter on a Sunday night and silently
thank the man who has granted me time to settle

into noiselessness long enough to find all the words
I least want to speak.

DISPATCH TO THE CRONE

Is the house quiet where you are?
Are all of the cabinet doors closed,

the drinking glasses unbroken
by the dog's karate-chop wagging tale

or your oldest's always-on-the-go
tendency to break things?

I imagine candles and music
at all hours. I imagine rooms

of sunlight, the curtains pulled back
because the TV isn't on so who cares

if there's a glare on the glass.
You stand by the counter cutting cheese,

dropping waxy crumble-crumbs
for the cat, and make a dinner

of the fancy crackers. You can do that
now. Time is wide, but ticking. Somewhere

your children are out there, past
the threshold you'd lock tight each night.

Their foreheads go unkissed, their backs
unscratched, their ears unhummed.

They drop into sleep without you,
they are dropping into their futures

without you, into lives where you will be
a faint memory, like the smell

of rosewater perfume or toothpaste
over coffee breath or clean sheets.

They propel their perfect, precious bodies
through days you can't fathom.

Your arms are weak with unhugging.
Your voice a hasp in your unwarmed

throat. You have longed for this emptiness,
haven't you? Don't tell me you're missing

the broken towel rack, the fart jokes
and heavy footfalls. Don't tell me

your life isn't full when it's only yours to fill.

DISPATCH ON THE GOLDEN RATIO

How long have I loved the pleasure of catching
and cataloguing the little beauties that flit past?

I snatch them from their own evanescence
and pin them through their living center.

They last a little longer—or forever—depending.
At any moment I can conjure inside myself

the paisley-shaped eyes my oldest son was given
by another woman, his smooth, almost boneless wrists,

tight curls that grow over the faintly downy rind
of his still-years-later-and-for-always-eminently-kissable

forehead. Little wonder when I found a body I craved
above all others, I conjured a copy of it in miniature.

Disbelief still, as I curl around my second son
and catalog the wide-palmed hands, end-jutting ribs,

balled calves, and gnome nose. I've worried at times
that my love for his father was only skin deep—the sight

of his sinuous arms tugging my hips towards him
locking and unlocking the clasp of my breathing,

the thirst-catch I can never quench no matter
how many kisses. For centuries his body

has sent artists scrambling towards a blankness
they needed to imprint with the felt permanence

of his perfection. Most of us aren't up to the task.
Two sculptors abandoned the block of marble

before Michelangelo coaxed my lover's legs
from that buttery rock. Polykleitos used his proportions

to invent geometry. Da Vinci inscribed his form
inside a circle, an image that echoes across centuries

like music of the spheres. He hardly knows
how to inhabit that heavenly body. Through

dappled forest and sun-glutted prairies, I watch
calves slip past the dip of opposite knee

like puzzle pieces. Once, he walked into a coffee shop
and tugged at his shirt hem as if he understood

the absurdity of his clothing, and I caught the flutter
of that image between my own two hands

and drove the pen in.

DISPATCH HALFWAY UP THE SUMMIT

When we finally left
the house, the state,

our two older children
with their other parents,

we took the child we'd made
to the mountains. As if

the slow climb against
fading light, the finding

of footing on early-season
snow, pines swiping

his eyes when we failed
to duck enough,

and view of time cutting
its shark-teeth on nothing

we can see, could save us
from the deep bruise

of numb months. All I know
about love is this: one foot,

another, head down, now stop
and look up. We carried him,

sleeping, up glacial scree,
and when he woke in that thin,

shifting air, he cried
at the height. I wanted him

to look on that expansiveness
and see how these bodies

keep us from being infinite.
But he is too new,

his stay still tenuous.
And bodies pressing

against their cages is how
he got here, anyway.

DISPATCH ON ETYMOLOGY

As in, explain yourself. As in, address without a clear
recipient. As in, transitive 1) to jot on envelopes, receipts,

over crayon scribbles I'm meant to treasure,
then pleat these words inside creases

bladed by fingernails, refolded to a point
for flight. Especially: furtively, in stolen minutes.

dispatch the day's small breaks and burns
As in 2) to splash crimson, quick flick of the paperknife,

to damper a flame in favor of waxy rivulets.
Obsolete: think better of. Obsolete: more silence.

Officer to *dispatch*, come in? As in 3) evasive action
needed, send reinforcements, report

on supplies, please advise. As in, the news
from here, no telling what condition

the destination or what's left of who sent this.
As in noun. As in, I'd send a body, if I could,

in place of words. As in 1) the static-crackle
clearing of a voice. *Hello? Can you hear me?*

Does anyone read me? Hello?

DISPATCH ON THE OBVIOUS

So many of the metaphors in this book
are too tidy, and perhaps this tells you

exactly what you need to know about me:
that you could be lying naked in my bed

and still I would not see that you want me.
That is something I could never believe.

I have always needed all the red string connecting
the evidence to convince me that my own mind

is trustworthy. So as I sat untangling a wad
of yarn, endless snarls that unraveled

to loose ends, I told my sister why I want
to write our estranged mother a letter

and cried. Yes, I know if our mother reads it, she might
be hurt and still not hear me. Yes, I know

better than to expect repair of a lifetime's unmended
breaks. Yes, I know my strangely steady hands

in the knotted and shredded remnants are too obvious
a metaphor for my relationship with my mother.

But this is what life handed me: a mother who never
convinced me I was lovable, and a mind that only sees

what's made too plain. The yarn is crude, hand-spun
into wavering thicknesses from two strands twisted

tight as helixes or airy as cotton candy—
lavender and cornflower, turquoise and amethyst—

and where one hue ends I can't tell you.
But I need for you to know the yarn is real.

I need you to believe me.

ACKNOWLEDGMENTS

- *Alaska Quarterly Review*—"Dispatch from the Beginning of the End" (a version of "Redacted Dispatch with Parenthetical Hindsight")
- *Atlanta Review*—"Dispatch from the Hotel Pool"
- *Another Chicago Magazine*—"Dispatch from the First Year Alone"
- *Barrow Street*—"Dispatch from a Petit Prelude"
- *Boulevard*—"Dispatch from a Viral Video"
- *Bright Bones: Contemporary Montana Writing*—"Dispatch from the Kmart Party Aisle," "Dispatch from a Failed Long Distance," "Dispatch from the Ars Poetica"
- *Calyx*—"Dispatch from That Day in Door County," "Dispatch from the Unwritten"
- *Crazyhorse*—"Dispatch from the Middle Distance"
- *The Heartland Review*—"Dispatch from a Familiar Fairy Tale," "Dispatch on the Golden Ratio"
- *The Hudson Review*—"Dispatch from the Storm Warning"
- *The MacGuffin*—"Dispatch Halfway Up the Summit"
- *Meridian*—"Dispatch from the Month Before Your Arrival"
- *Mother Egg Review*—"Dispatch from a Memory of Mint," "Dispatch from Another Familiar Fairy Tale"
- *Poet Lore*—"Dispatch in the Form of an Epilogue or Prologue"
- *The Pinch*—"Dispatch from the Fairy Tale's Retelling"
- *The Practicing Poet*—"Dispatch from the Middle Distance"
- *Salamander*—"Dispatch from Your Fourth Month"
- *Willow Springs*—"Dispatch from Simultaneous Swim Lessons," "Dispatch Four Days After the Funeral"

"Dispatch from the Domestic Interior" was commissioned by Ally Wilber for the art exhibition "Claiming Space" at the Museum of Wisconsin Art, July 24-October 3, 2021. It borrows an image from Lauren Semivan's painting, "Low Tide."

I am grateful to Amy Ratto Parks, Freesia McKee, Rachel May, Leigh Feld, Austin Segrest, Steve Bellin-Oka, Ron Mohring, Veronica Golos, Will Barnes, Wayne Johns, and Jeremy Knaus for donating their time to read many of these poems. I am grateful to Trinica Sampson for offering feedback as a sensitivity reader, and to Callista Buchen for her thoughts on the manuscript as a whole.

"Dispatch from the First Year Alone" is copied from a letter to B.S.

In "Dispatch from the Ars Poetica," the words "nature's first green-gold" is cribbed from a line in Robert Frost's "Nothing Gold Can Stay."

In "Dispatch from a *New York Times* Article the Day Mary Oliver Died," the lines in italics are from various Mary Oliver poems. The poem references imagery from an article published in *The New York Times* on January 17, 2019, by Max Paradiso, entitled "To Save the Sound of a Stradivarius, a Whole City Must Keep Quiet."

ABOUT THE AUTHOR

Megan Gannon is the author of *Cumberland* (a novel) and *White Nightgown* (poems). Her work has appeared in *Best American Poetry, Ploughshares, Pleiades,* and most recently in *Alaska Quarterly Review, Atlanta Review, Calyx, Meridian,* and *The Pinch*. She is an associate professor of English at Ripon College in Wisconsin.